A Gold Christmas

Gold Hockey #14

Elise Faber

A GOLD CHRISTMAS
BY ELISE FABER
Newsletter sign-up

A GOLD CHRISTMAS
Copyright © 2021 Elise Faber
Print ISBN-13: 978-1-63749-048-8
Ebook ISBN-13: 978-1-63749-047-1
Cover Art by Jena Brignola

Gold Hockey Series

Gold Cast of Characters

Heroes and Heroines:

Brit Plantain (Blocked) — first female goalie in the NHL, loves boy bands

Stefan Barie (Blocked) — captain of the Gold

Sara Jetty (Backhand) — artist and figure skater

Mike Stewart (Backhand) —defenseman for the Gold, romance guru

Blane Hart (Boarding) — center for the Gold, number 22

Mandy Shallows (Boarding) — trainer and physical therapist

Max Montgomery (Benched) — defensemen for the Gold, giant nerd

Angelica Shallows (Benched) — engineer at RoboTech, also a giant nerd

Blue Anderson (Breakaway) — top forward in the league and for the Gold

Anna Hayes (Breakaway) — Max's former nanny, no relation to Kevin Hayes

Rebecca Stravokraus (Breakout) — Gold publicist, makes killer brownies, known at PR-Rebecca

Kevin Hayes (Breakout) — forward for the Gold, no relation to Anna Hayes

Rebecca Hallbright (Checked) — nutritionist for the Gold, plethora of delicious vegan recipes, known as Nutrionist-Rebecca

Gabe Carter (Checked) — doctor, head trainer for the Gold

Calle Stevens (Coasting) — assistant coach for the Gold, former national team member

Coop Armstrong (Coasting) — talented forward on the Gold, addicted to historical romance audiobooks

Mia Caldwell (Centered) — 5th degree black belt, brings the snark

Liam Williamson (Centered) — Gold forward finding his love for the game, charming and pushy in equal measures

Charlotte Harris (Charging) — new Gold GM, hates losing and the game Chubby Bunny

Logan Walker (Charging) — defensemen for the Gold, skills include: cockiness and being able to buy presents that make Charlotte squirm

Dani Eastbrook (Caged) — video coach for the Gold, tech nerd, could fix your computer in a flash, shy

Ethan Korhonen (Caged) — forward for the Gold, killer power play skills, known as Big Juicy Brain

Fanny Douglas (Crashed) — silver medalist, skating coach for the Gold

Brandon Cunningham (Crashed) — brown curls, penchant for hallways, Kaydon Lewis's agent

Kaydon Lewis (Cycled) — yummy stubble, great with kids, doesn't mind a little snot

Scarlett Andrews (Cycled) — quiet, perfectionist, resembled Bambi on ice

Devon Scott (Block & Tackle) — former player, current owner Prestige Media group

Becca Scott (Block & Tackle) — Devon's assistant

Additional Characters:
Charlie Andrews — Scarlett's brother

Bernard — head coach

Richie — equipment manager

Dan Plantain — Brit's brother

Diane Barie — Stefan's mom

Pierre Barie — Stefan's dad, owner of the Gold

Spence — former goalie, married to Monique, daughter Mirabel

Monique — married to Spence, former model

Mirabel — daughter of Spence and Monique

Mitch — Sara's boss

Allison and Sean — Blane's parents

Pascal — Devon Scott's security lead

Roger Shallows — Mandy's dad

Grant and Megan — Devon's parents

ONE

BRIT

There was a stampede closing in on her.

Or, well, less stampede and more like a trio of six-feet-plus, two-hundred-and-odd-pound men speeding to her, albeit gracefully. The roar of the crowd quieting until she could hear sounds of their skates crunching on the ice, the smacks of their sticks, the calls between the players of their opponent that evening.

She didn't have a lot of time, hence the thoughts of stampedes.

Her eyes flicked past the trio to find her defensemen too far behind to catch up—she sure as shit was going to give Blane a hard time for the bungled play later (in the vein of a friend who'd known him almost her entire life), but right now she had to focus.

On hockey.

On making sure these fuckers didn't score because it was late in the game and her team was up by a goal, and she wanted to go home and be with her husband, not play overtime and potentially have to be in net for a shootout.

Where players went one-on-one against the goalie (against her) and she had to shut them down.

Not her favorite, even though she generally thrived on high stakes and high intensity.

Kind of like right *now*.

Taking a deep breath, she focused, time seeming to slow to a crawl.

It gave her the ability to take in every detail, to see that Blane would make it back in time to cover the player at the top of the circles. The other two were on her, nearer the net and the bigger threat.

She came out of her net, challenging the man with the puck, hoping to force a pass early—or in an ideal world, for him to bungle and break up the whole play. Though in truth, these guys were too good for it to end that simply, and nearly the moment she challenged, she had to scramble.

The puck sailed to the other player, forcing her to dig in her edges to lunge to close the angle, to cut off the open net so it wasn't an easy tap-home goal.

If he'd shot the moment he'd received the pass, he probably could have scored.

But he held on to it a second too long before shooting, and she made the stop, the puck rebounding off her pads. She kicked her leg, trying to direct it to the corner, but it hit a piece of ice or a divot or . . . fuck, maybe the hockey gods were just screwing with her. Regardless, it didn't quite make it that far, instead drifting to the No Man's Land—too far for her to reach, too near the net to not be a real threat.

"Fuck," she hissed, scrambling again, lurching ungracefully to the side and having to make a last-ditch effort by stacking her pads.

A risk because it took her off her feet, slowed her ability to get up and move. As the only female goalie in the league, she was agile and smaller than the other goalies; her strength was her agility.

Thus, making snow angels on the ice was *not* her way.

It worked this time, though.

The puck hit her in the stomach, knocking the wind out of her, sending a burning pain through her torso. But that wasn't the first time, nor the last she would scramble with her lungs screaming for air.

She flopped again, a fish ashore attempting to lurch its way back into the lake, and covered the puck.

Then sent a little mental offering to the hockey gods when the whistle blew, and she was able to crawl to her skates and just breathe for a moment.

"Fuck," she muttered, tossing the biscuit to the ref before turning to grab a sip of water. She wasn't particularly thirsty, but she did need a minute for the sting of the puck hitting her stomach to subside. The disc of black vulcanized rubber seemed to have an uncanny ability to wriggle its way in between pads, to find the few vulnerable inches of skin. In this case, the small strip of flesh that had been exposed between her hockey pants and her chest protector, with only her jersey remaining in place to act as insulation.

Hence the burning, motherfucker that it was.

Good times.

Blane tapped her with his stick, asking, "You good?"

She nodded. "Good."

"I owe you one," he said.

The pain was subsiding, and she could see he felt like shit about the play, so she forced a smile and winked. "Damn right, you do."

He shook his head, tapped her again, and then skated to the bench for a change. Brit dropped her bottle back onto the top of the net, bobbed her chin so her helmet slid back down over her face, then picked up her stick and got ready for the puck to drop.

Her gaze drifted to the clock. Two and a half minutes to go.

Time to get this shit done.

———

She hissed in pain when she shifted to yank her jersey over her head, tossing it into the bin that had been rolled into the center of the locker room for the equipment team to take care of.

They hadn't gotten shit done.

Or at least not in regulation. Or in overtime.

They *had* gotten it done in the shootout. She'd stopped two of three, and Blue, Liam, and Coop had all scored. They'd won the game. A little later than planned, but the two points were theirs.

At this point in the season, a woman had to take her victories where she got them.

They were on a solid bid to take back the lead of the conference, though there was quite a bit of season left in front of them to keep it. Still, they were only two weeks from Christmas, ten games left for the year, and they were currently trailing first place by four points. Which meant they had a real shot at catching up, at pulling ahead before the new year rang in, and they'd have an entire week off to reset for the push of the back side of the season. The break would be good. Many of them were tired and sore, and a couple of the guys were injured—the side effect of an eighty-two-game season in a brutal sport like hockey. The game was full of hits and checks, fights and collisions, as well as the normal wear-and-tear on the human body that came from pushing it to its limits. But all of that physicality caught up eventually, no matter how good their support staff was, especially when they'd had to fight like hell for every win so far this season, and the intensity of gameplay seemed to be increasing by the minute.

Luckily for Brit, she just needed some bruise cream, a soak in the hot and cold tubs, and a long bath when she got home, and she'd be right as rain.

Some of the other guys were going to be rehabbing much longer.

Blane slid onto the bench next to her, regret on his face that had her elbowing him. "Stop," she said. "Shit happens." She knew she'd promised herself that she was going to give her friend a hard time, but she hated to see that defeated expression. "It's fine."

"You sure?"

She slugged him. Not gently either. "I'm sure."

"Great." He straightened, brown eyes filled with something that looked like amusement. "Then I *won't* give you my day on the radio."

"What?" Brit snagged the back of his hockey pants, hauling him to a stop. "You don't get to do take-backsies on that."

"Technically, I didn't *give* it yet."

"Well, I'm taking it." Blane's day on the radio—not really the radio, but rather in charge of the locker room's playlist—was tomorrow, and torturing the guys with her favorite sappy, saccharine pop music would be the absolute best therapy for that night's game.

Plus, giving someone their radio day was like giving them a truckload of gold bullion.

It was the gesture of all gestures.

She very much accepted.

"Shake on it," she said, extending her hand, wanting to institute the time-honored—and *only*—tradition that would pass on the sacred tradition of radio control from one player to another.

Blane kept his hands firmly at his sides.

"Don't do it," Coop called. "No guilt is worth Brit having music control."

She jabbed a finger in his direction. "I'm your goalie. You're supposed to keep me happy."

Coop smirked. "That's Stefan's job."

She tossed her glove at him. Which he caught, of course. Fucking athletes with their excellent hand-eye coordination. He blew her a kiss.

Which had her lifting her middle finger in a very delicate, ladylike gesture of goodwill. Also, "Fuck you," she called.

He tossed her glove back, which she caught, thank *her* excellent hand-eye coordination skills. Mentally, she blew on her knuckles, buffed them on her shoulder. "Love you, Brit," Coop said.

She glared, but she loved him too. She loved *all* the big lugs. They were her family—a family that could be a major pain in the ass, for sure—but she cared about them enough to push them out of the way of an oncoming car, to occasionally throw a rock song into her playlist on her radio days, even to hang behind if they were all being chased by a grizzly bear and fight the ursine off with her own bare hands.

Well, she'd probably be able to outrun it.

Or at least that's what the boys always said when she was leading their asses in their joint workouts, blazing ahead of them even though they moved like liquid lightning on the ice.

Still, just because she loved them didn't mean that she was going to let Blane get away with offering extra music privileges up like they were a carrot on a stick. She reached up, conducted some very sneaky moves to manipulate his hand into a handshake.

"Ha!" she exclaimed when his hand instinctively tightened. "The mantle has been passed!" She did a little dance.

"Thief," he said, eyes filled with mirth.

She made a face, not stopping her dance, which no doubt looked ridiculous since she was still half-dressed in her equipment. "You were going to offer it."

He swatted her, shaking his head at her antics, then hooked his arm around her neck and tugged her close for a hug. "You're a pain in my ass," he grumbled, kissing the top of her head like the surrogate big brother he'd been her whole life. "But I love you anyway." He released her. "Enjoy the radio day." A beat. "I—and everyone else—will be gouging our eyes out."

Her brows dragged together. "And by eyes, I hope you mean ears?"

"Ears," he confirmed then grinned. "But eyes would certainly make it more interesting for you in net."

Her lips twitched, but she pressed them flat, glared. "I hate it when things get interesting."

"Lie." He punched her in the shoulder. "Great game tonight. You saved us, as always."

"Meh." She sank back down onto the bench, started untying her skates. "Can't score all that easily from my end of the ice."

"You could try," he said, moving to his spot a few places down.

"You'll clear the net?" she asked. "Give me an easy shot?"

"If you'll stop being lazy and just hanging around in our goal." He managed to keep a straight face, even though she balled her dirty sock and tossed it at him. Swooping it off the ground, he said, "God knows, we could use another stick in the offensive zone sometimes. Fuckers can barely score," he said, raising his voice as he tossed the balled-up sock into the bin in the middle and subsequently ignoring the hisses and boos from the forwards, dodging even more socks and spheres of compressed tape thrown in his direction at his slight hit.

More good-natured insults were lobbed.

Ribbing was dished out about Blane's inability to handle the puck and his skill at causing three-on-ones, and . . .

God, she loved these guys.

Her job was the absolute best in the world.

Two

STEFAN

He stood inside the training suite, his shoulder against one wall while the woman who held his heart in her palm talked with Mandy, the trainer for the Gold.

Pride blossomed inside him as he watched them. They were both extremely smart and capable, and he felt lucky to know them. But he was only in love with one of them, was only hanging out in a room he'd retired from visiting several years before because his wife was here.

Otherwise, he'd be home in his Old Man Pants—thanks to Brit for that name for his favorite pair of ratty sweatpants—a beer in one hand, a gooey, sugary dessert from his secret stash in the other.

But he was here.

Watching the woman he loved.

Sans beer and sugary desserts because she was on a strict diet plan and because he followed it with her.

One because, without the physical exertion of hockey, he didn't want to balloon up—he did have a sexy-as-sin wife with a fabulous body to stay in shape for. Last thing he needed was for her to leave him for a younger, more attractive rookie. Which, obviously, he was joking. Brit didn't care what he looked like, just as he didn't care about her appearance. He followed the diet because it made him feel good, and also because he didn't want to make following the plan any harder on Brit by eating things around her or having stuff in the house that was just providing temptation. Stefan understood from personal experience that the job was tough as hell, and he wanted to be supportive in any way he could.

Even if that included hanging around his old stomping grounds and walking by pictures of him during his time as captain that felt like they'd happened just yesterday, even though it had been years now since he'd retired from playing.

He probably could have secured another contract, been skating for the Gold or some other team, but . . . he'd been done.

He wanted time to work on other projects, to do something besides living and breathing hockey, so after the team had won the Cup, he hadn't gone looking for extensions. He'd finished his contract then retired.

And now, he was Brit's number one fan in the stands.

Which was sometimes harder than expected—especially when he felt like he could do a better job on the ice or when Brit was left unprotected or got hit or was injured. Okay, during those times, it was absolutely miserable to be sitting and not participating, especially when his only pastime at the moment was sitting on the board of the Gold's charity and twiddling his thumbs.

And since their plans for adopting had stalled in a painful limbo . . .

He needed to find something to do.

"Hey."

Stefan blinked and glanced up from his shoes, every cell in his body calming instinctively as though Brit were a miracle salve smoothed over all the rough, aching edges inside him. "Hey," he murmured, running the backs of his knuckles over her cheek.

"Good game." He pressed a light kiss to her lips then fought a smile. "I know how much you love shootouts."

She rolled her beautiful brown eyes. "That I do. So, *so* much." She studied him for a moment. "If you're tired, you can go. I'll just meet you at home."

Normally, he waited until she was done with her post-game routine, following her car on the nights he didn't drive her in. So typically, he would have rebuffed her offer, told her he wasn't tired, that he'd wait as long as it took.

Because he liked being with her, even if it was just hanging on the sidelines while she did her thing.

Tonight, however, he *was* tired.

Tonight, he was unsettled and needed . . .

Something.

He nodded, brushed his knuckles over her cheek again. "I'll see you at home."

An emotion flitted across her face, there and gone before he could decipher it, but then she pressed a kiss to his cheek, said, "I'll be there soon."

"Take your time."

She hesitated, her teeth nibbling into her bottom lip. "Stef—"

"Brit!" Mandy called. "Get your cute butt over here! I'm not done with you yet. Muhaha!"

She turned, her blond ponytail flitting behind her, waved at Mandy as though to say, *"Just a minute,"* then spun back to face him. "Baby, are you—?"

"Brit!" Mandy yelled again. "There's no getting out of my torture!"

His wife sighed. "I swear to God, if she wasn't so good at her job . . ."

"Go," he murmured. "I'm good. I promise. Just tired."

She held his eyes for one more moment then nodded, squeezed his hand, and went over to The Force of Nature—a.k.a. Mandy. Stefan slipped out of the training suite, walked through the halls of the arena that had been his home for years, and moved through the parking lot to his car.

It was a quiet night, the stars twinkling overhead in between tendrils of ocean fog drifting in from the Pacific. The bite of the cool air felt good on his skin, soothing in a way that the cold of the ice hitting his face used to settle him just before he stepped onto the rink.

But all too soon, he was in the quiet of his car, and the stifling feeling of not having something meaningful to *do* bore down on him.

He had meaningful *people* in his life. He was lucky to have his mom, Brit, Blane, Mike, Blue, Max, not to mention the Force of Nature herself, Mandy, both Rebeccas, and so many others. His life was full.

It was just . . . he was standing still. Watching.

Wanting to start a family.

But . . . Brit.

Not that she didn't want to start one, too. She did. For sure. They both were ready to turn the page, to begin the story of that next adventure. But, for obvious reasons, she couldn't get pregnant right then, not with pucks being shot at her and hockey players occasionally ending up in the net with her.

So, they'd decided to adopt.

Not because it was a second choice, or because it was a last resort, but because when one of her teammates had suggested it, adoption had seemed to fit perfectly.

They'd begun the process.

But it had *just* begun. Brit had come home with the idea, something obvious and that made total sense for them. They had the resources to adopt, the space to foster, and Stefan had kicked himself for not recognizing it sooner. Because now they were waiting for their application to be approved by the state *and* they were waiting for someone to choose them through the adoption agency, like they were lined up in the back of a room with a slew of other hopeful parents hoping that someone would pick them for their team.

He'd been picked his whole life.

And now, for the last two months . . . nothing.

Which, look, he got it was ridiculous to be upset. Two months was no time at all. It was just . . . he was impatiently waiting to fill a hole inside him and—

"Enough," Stefan murmured, clenching his fingers on his steering wheel.

He needed to be patient, to focus his energy on something else. He was a firm believer in things happening in their own time. This would work out when the time was right. Stefan just needed . . .

Something.

Brit had gone back to the glorious distraction of hockey. He'd thrown himself into the charity, but that was hardly enough to fill his days, and he was hesitant to take on more in case . . .

It happened.

They were picked and—

Sighing, he took the offramp, driving up to their house, secluded in a gated community on the far edge of town. The neighborhood was quiet, with lots of green space and a highly rated elementary school.

He knew because he'd looked.

He knew because he'd researched even before they bought the place.

He knew because he'd understood even when they were first married that one day, they would be starting a family.

But now, his life felt like it was stuck on pause.

"Patience," he murmured, hitting the garage door clicker as he pulled into the driveway. This would all work out. It would all be okay. He just needed to breathe and chill the fuck out and remember that the most important things were Brit and his mom, his friends. Hell, he'd even managed to repair things—mostly—

with his dad. This hiccup would pass, and then they would move on with their lives, with adding to their family.

The garage door slid closed, and he moved into the house, disarming the alarm, flicking on a few more lights, and then despite it not being a Cheat Day, he grabbed a beer, opened it, and took it to the back patio.

Staring up at the sky, he sipped his beer, determined to stop moping and to focus on all the things he knew he should be grateful for—including but not limited to having lots of people in his life he loved and cared about and who loved and cared for him right back, as well as a place to live in a safe neighborhood, electricity and internet and food in the fridge, and all the wonderful people in his life were healthy and happy. His problems were small, were those of the privileged, and he needed to stop whining about it. Because he was lucky.

He was so *damned* lucky.

Sighing, he stared up at the sky and knew that if he thought it enough, it would sink in.

THREE

BRIT

She pulled next to Stefan's car in the garage and couldn't stop the sinking feeling in her stomach from expanding when she stepped into the house and saw all the lights were off.

Silly, but she'd thought he would wait up for her.

Like he always did.

But he wasn't waiting up.

She padded across the kitchen, got herself a glass of water, then headed upstairs into their bedroom, her gaze automatically sliding past the closed door in the hall as she moved. That door had remained closed from the moment they'd cleared the space out two months back, from the moment they had prepared it to welcome a child.

They hadn't filled it yet, not with a crib or a bed, not with clothes or toys.

Because they didn't know who they would be welcoming yet. A baby? Hopefully. Older children. Hopefully, them as well. They had several empty rooms in the hall, but none they'd cleared out yet, thinking they'd start with one child and that they'd add more kids once they got their feet wet.

This was new and a huge responsibility. They'd wanted to start small.

She kept walking, slipping into her and Stefan's bedroom, and moving quietly until she saw the bed was empty. When the bathroom and closet also both proved to be empty, she headed back downstairs, through the kitchen, and out onto the back patio.

There he was.

Sitting quietly in one of their chairs, so still and quiet she might have assumed he was asleep. Except, Brit knew her husband.

He wasn't asleep.

He was troubled.

She wasn't stupid enough to have missed it, even though he'd tried to hide it.

Unfortunately, it wasn't something she knew how to solve.

Because *she* was the reason they'd gone the route of adoption, of fostering. Because if she had a different job, if she was a different woman, they'd be on the road to having a family, and they wouldn't be stuck in this limbo.

She crossed over to him, sinking onto his lap. "Hi, baby," she whispered.

His arms came around her, his forehead resting on her shoulder. "You played great tonight."

"Thanks," she whispered, holding him tight, struggling to find the words.

Everything was okay when she was on the ice, when she was in the locker room with the guys. But when that shield was gone, she felt . . .

Her fault.

This limbo, the empty ache, was her fault, and she didn't know how to fix it.

She could keep pucks out of the net. She could work hard on

her glove hand, do her level best to win games for her team, but she couldn't solve this . . . unless—

"I won't sign the next contract," she whispered. "I'll stop, so we can—"

Stefan went ramrod stiff, and the next second, she was on her feet, him towering over her. "No," he said fiercely. "No *fucking* way."

"I—" She shook her head. "What if no one picks us? What if our application for the license isn't approved because I'm away playing so much? I can't solve this for us when I'm play—"

"This isn't for *you* to solve," he said, cupping her cheeks in both of his palms. "No, sweetheart. I don't want that. I just . . ." His voice cracked.

"Want our life after hockey to begin," she whispered.

His throat worked, and he was quiet for a long time, his hands tense. "No," he eventually said, and she saw a flicker of determination drift across his eyes. "Our life has *already* begun. I'm sorry, I've been impatient." He tucked her hair behind her ear. "I'm sorry, I've been off. I just thought it was going to happen right away. I've gotten too used to instant gratification"—the ghost of a smile—"So now, I'm going to focus on other things because I know it'll happen when it happens."

"But—"

"*And*," he said, talking over her in a way that was uncommon, because her husband might be able to give a soundbite to the media with the best of them, but he was also a man who listened more than he spoke. Well, that and he oftentimes didn't get a *chance* to speak, what with his chattering wife who always had a comment about something. "And," he said again, "I don't ever want you to think that I want you to change who you are. You decide when you're done, not me, not someone else." He tapped her chest, just above her heart. "This'll tell you." The corner of his mouth turned up. "And then you'll tell me, okay?"

Brit swallowed hard, sort of hating that she'd been trying to comfort him, and in the end, he'd comforted her. But that was the kind of man Stefan was. He thought of others, was kind and compassionate. He was too damned good sometimes, and she loved him so fucking much for it. "Okay," she murmured, promising herself she'd do everything in her power to make this happen for him, to ensure that she gave him as much love and comfort as he so freely doled out.

"Good," he said then took her hand, tugged her toward the house. "You need to be in bed and resting up." His fingers trailed lightly across her abdomen. "How's the bruise?"

"Fine."

A brow lifted as he secured the door. "Mandy say it was fine?"

She rolled her eyes. "Mandy worries too much. Plus, we have tomorrow off. I'll slather on the cream a couple more times, and I won't even feel it the next time I'm on the ice."

"Hmm."

She narrowed her eyes. "Hmm, what?"

He tugged her up the stairs, fingers trailing along her side now, drifting higher. "*Hmm,* as in, maybe you can't reach the right spot, and I should be the one to put that cream on for you."

Amusement bubbled within her. "Because I need supervision to put it on my stomach?"

A nod, his blue eyes filled with humor. He drew them to a stop at the foot of the bed. "Definitely. You can't do anything to your body without supervision."

Her lips curved, a giggle bubbling up in her throat when she saw the mischief in his expression. She turned to face him, stepped close. "Maybe I also need to take off all my clothes, so you can make sure I don't have other bruises somewhere else?"

Heat kindled on his face. "You'll *definitely* need to be naked, otherwise I won't be able to stroke all those different places."

"Hmm." She toed off her shoes. "Is applying bruise cream considered stroking?"

"It is the way I do it." He reached for the button on his jeans, flicked. "I also happen to need to be naked, as well."

"Oh?" Brit began unbuttoning her shirt, parting it down the

middle before unzipping her slacks. "That helps you apply the cream?"

His hands guided the plain white cotton down her shoulders, off her hands. "Most definitely," he said, running those slightly rough, warm palms along her skin as he tugged her close and undid the clasp of her bra.

She tilted her head to the side, felt his mouth close over the sensitive spot just beneath her jaw, making her shiver and melt against him, turning her into a pile of mush. Stefan was the only one who could ever do that, the only one who could make her forget about everything except the feel of his body, the sensations he wrought in hers, the love in her heart, and the desire that made every part of her tremble.

Her pants hit the carpet, and then she was on her back on the mattress, a naked Stefan poised over her. His mouth found hers, his tongue delving deep, his hands drifting over her body, cupping her breasts, skating along her sides, dipping in between her thighs. She moaned, hips canting, clit throbbing, aching to be touched.

Lips on her skin, between her legs, sliding through damp heat, his tongue making her tremble and grind against his mouth. Then he slipped a finger inside, curling it up in the way that never failed to send sparks of pleasure down her spine. She moaned, shattered, riding his lips and tongue as pleasure yanked her under its writhing eddies.

Limp, her head flopped back onto her pillow.

A moment later, Stefan was spreading her legs wider, rising up on his knees between them. He pressed home, making her lips part on a contented moan, and then he was moving, and it was fucking glorious. Her hands gripped his shoulders, holding tight to the hard muscles, listening to his rapid breaths as he stroked deep. Gorgeous. The man was absolutely beautiful, especially with a sheen of sweat on his skin, with his face drawn tight, determination and heat, pleasure and need filling his deep brown eyes.

Her pleasure lifted, twining higher and spiraling tighter,

carrying her up into space, orbiting, spinning out of control until . . . she exploded like a meteor hitting the outer atmosphere.

Stefan kept moving, sparking new levels of ecstasy, until she was a giant sweaty lump of woman, melting into the mattress, her lids beyond heavy.

If some tiny sprite had hooked concrete blocks to her eyelashes, she wouldn't have been surprised. As it was, she just lay there while Stefan went to the bathroom, washed up, then came back in and cleaned her up. When he pulled her close, tucking the covers up and over them, she snuggled against his chest and let sleep come.

Four

Stefan

"This one?" he asked, resting the saw against his thigh and surveying the tall pine tree, its branches and needles in seemingly perfect arrangement.

At least in his male eyes.

Brit slid her arm through his, her breast brushing against his triceps, making his cock twitch. God, he wanted this woman. That burning need for her had never waned. She said his name, looked at him sideways, accidentally brushed one of his favorite body parts—her breasts, though he'd be lying if he said he didn't love them all—against his arm again.

She studied the tree, pursed her lips together, and they'd been married long enough for him to already know this tree wouldn't pass muster.

He began moving through the aisle of the lot full of Douglas firs, eyes scouring the spiny green conifers for what he thought his wife would consider the perfect Christmas evergreen.

Then stopped, her body brushing against his again. "This one?" he asked.

She released his arm, made a circle around the tree, gaze

searching high and low, studying every branch carefully. Would there be lip pursing? Or would there be—

His breath caught.

Because no lip pursing was present. Instead, she was smiling, and it was fucking beautiful. That smile had been the first thing he'd noticed about her—how it lit up a room, her inner beauty shining through, making him feel as though he'd just swallowed the sun and it had filled him with warmth.

"It's perfect," she said, holding her hand up. "Saw, please."

A tug of her ponytail. "Nope." He crouched, crawled in beneath the bottom branches. "Gotta rest those arms for the game tomorrow."

She snorted. "Stefan."

"Plus," he said, sliding across the damp earth and positioning the saw against the trunk, "this way, you'll get to look at my ass."

Laughter filled the air, and he watched her boots until they drifted out of sight, the crunching on the ground telling him that she was moving behind him, shifting very close, until her palm cupped said ass, nearly making him slice off a finger when she drifted it forward just enough for him to stop thinking about his butt and to start thinking about his cock.

Her voice was soft, laced with humor and heat. "You know what I say about hockey players and their asses," she murmured, her fingers tapping just above the button of his jeans.

"Tease," he grumbled.

"Damn right," she said, "and you love it."

He did love it, but instead of giving her the satisfaction of admitting that, he grunted and kept sawing.

"For the record, hockey players have the best asses." She moved closer, though unfortunately it was to grab the trunk above him, steadying the tree while he sawed like a motherfucker, wanting to throw her over his shoulder and take her back to their house, to embrace their day off by worshipping every inch of her body.

But they had a tree to decorate, lights to put up, Christmas spirit to invoke.

It had become one of their favorite holidays, a break in the busy season to just veg out and watch *Die Hard* (because, of course, they needed to include Brit's favorite holiday movie in their vegging). They'd forget about the diet plan for a day (maybe even go hog wild and forget about it for two), drink hot chocolate and cider, gorge on cookies. He'd have some eggnog while Brit gagged, and they'd go over to his mom's house for dinner. The only drawback would be his dad being there, but that was less of a negative than it used to be.

The fucker was growing on him.

And since Pierre was making his mom happy, Stefan had promised to bury the hatchet. In all avenues, the old man was trying, and the least he could do was try, too, especially when it made his mom's life better.

In the meantime, though, he had sawing to do.

The trunk was thicker than it looked, or maybe the blade was dull, but either way, he was sweating like a pig before he was done, covered in needles and sawdust, the dampness of the ground soaking in through his jeans.

"Need some help, Old Man?" Brit teased.

He grunted, kept sawing.

She laughed, tilted the tree enough that the blade stopped getting stuck, making it much easier for the blade to move.

"Teamwork?" he muttered.

"Makes the dream work," she quipped, shifting to snag the tree so it didn't crash over when he made it through the final inch.

He jumped to his feet.

Her lips parted, eyes warm, the teasing flitting away. "You did good, baby," she whispered.

"It's just a tree," he said.

"No," she said. "It's not." Her hand rested on his chest, her body drifted close. "It's you. I love you, so much." He wound his free arm around her hips, bringing her flush against him. Her eyes darted around. "Stef, someone might see—"

He dropped the saw. "Don't care."

Her lips curved, her free arm slid up his arm, over his shoulder, to his nape, and wound into his hair. "Good," she murmured. "Because I don't, either."

She rose on tiptoe. He bent.

And then their mouths aligned, and he was kissing the woman he loved.

That night, they made the local news, their bodies pressed together, their lips locked and . . . the perfect Christmas tree in the background.

It was the first time he'd ever printed off a paparazzi picture and stuck it to the fridge.

Lucky.

Yeah, he was so damned lucky.

Even when his wife made him rehang the strands of lights no less than five times.

FIVE

BRIT

He was behind her net.

It was funny how she could always feel his gaze on her, how it was a warm and comforting weight. No judgment if a puck went in the net. But worry in his eyes if she took a hit. A smile, a small nod if she made a good save.

When he'd been on the team, he'd always tapped her pads with his stick after the whistle. Now, she felt those taps when he caught her gaze through the glass.

But it had been two months—almost three!—since they'd filled out their foster parent application, the same amount of time since they'd selected an adoption agency, and they heard . . . crickets.

Nothing.

No additional requests for paperwork.

Well, that wasn't a hundred percent true. They'd had an interview and a home inspection right after both applications were in.

But nothing since.

Their lawyer said, in this case, no news was good news. They hadn't been rejected from becoming foster parents, everything was just in process via that course, and the adoption agency just hadn't matched them with anyone yet. But . . . here, they'd been worried about what might happen if both fronts had worked out, how they'd manage with a full house and knowing it would be awesome, even as they'd patted themselves on the back, thinking themselves so smart for working from multiple angles, especially when they'd be happy with either route. And instead . . . disappointment.

"You're being ridiculous, Plantain," she muttered to herself, skating a loop behind the back of the net to stretch her legs. "It hasn't even been three months. These things take time." She knew that. Their lawyer and the agencies had warned them. Their research had confirmed the fact.

It was just . . . patience wasn't her strong suit.

And Stefan was so fucking good, so freaking supportive and amazing. *He* was patient, was trying to put on a good show, pretending he wasn't worried or anxious about starting their family, and meanwhile, she could feel that impulse roiling under the surface of his skin.

Dammit.

She wanted to solve it for him.

She wanted to make him as happy as he made her and—

The whistle blew. She sucked in a breath as the players lined up, readied herself in the net, and focused.

The puck dropped.

———

She winced when Mandy rotated her shoulder. "You're lucky there's only one more game before the break."

"Yup," Brit said. "Because I can definitely tough my way—"

"Through sitting on the bench while Harrison takes the start," Mandy finished for her. "Your rotation sucks," she added when Brit would have protested. "You need to rest this, and I will make that an order, if need be, including scratching your ass.

Otherwise, I can tell Bernard to start Harry and not complain if you happen to get put into the game at some point."

"But—"

"A full game is out of the question." She narrowed her eyes. "And I'm only agreeing to the potential of a period or two because you have the break coming up."

Christmas in three days.

Only one game in the week between the holiday and New Year's, and then, somehow, a full seven days without any matchups after the first.

Probably because they had a brutal month after that, with an extended road trip plus several home-and-home games against two of the other California teams—the Sharks and the Kings.

Then it would be the final push to the playoffs.

She couldn't wait.

"You with me?" Mandy asked.

Brit nodded, albeit begrudgingly.

"Good." Mandy patted her shoulder—not the sore one—and then went to talk to Blue, whose expression she thought, appeared as equally begrudging as Brit's own must have.

Stefan leaned a hip next to her on the padded table, his blue eyes dancing. "The Force strikes again?"

She stuck out her bottom lip. "I'm not starting the next game."

He knew her well enough to not sling platitudes—no, "It'll be fine" or "You need the rest" or the dreaded, "It's for the best" or "It's the right call"—instead, he just slipped his arm around her and pulled her in for a quick hug.

"Let's go home," he murmured. "I picked up your favorite from Molly's for your Cheat Day tomorrow."

See what she meant about Stefan being the best?

She hugged him back then nodded, pushing up from the table and lacing her fingers through her husband's, and when he had her favorite post-game playlist cued up to blare through the speakers on his car the moment he turned on the engine, hit the button for her seat-warmer before she could reach for it herself, Brit couldn't help but feel like the scales were constantly tipped in her direction.

He was just heaping on the caring, and all she'd done that week was make him dinner.

Which she'd burned.

Ugh.

She needed to do better. She needed to do something. She needed—

"I smell smoke."

Blinking, she asked, "You do?"

"Yeah." She saw the corner of his mouth curve up. "You're thinking hard enough to start a forest fire."

"You're not funny."

"That's not what you said last night," he teased.

"That's *exactly* what I said last night," she pushed back.

He rested his hand on her thigh. "Maybe I'm remembering wrong," he said silkily. "Maybe it was you moaning for more last night."

Her legs tightened, pleasure lancing through her. She *had* been moaning for more the night before, because Stefan and his glorious tongue and cock had made it his goal to make her come as many times as possible before she collapsed into a heap of useless muscles and bones.

Four.

It had been four orgasms before she'd cried off.

Four might be her new favorite number ever.

Still, she was herself, which meant that she didn't just give in or admit things like the fact that she had been reduced to a useless heap by her loving husband, even if it was true. Instead, she gave back sass. Because she was competitive, because she and Stefan liked to tease each other. Because life was more fun when they weren't serious all the time.

"Maybe I was moaning because I hated it."

Okay, not her best comeback.

But it wasn't her fault.

Stefan's hand had slid up, was pressing between her legs, the seam a delicious pressure as it found her clit.

Her words had him bursting into laughter, his hand, sadly, sliding free. "Well, I won't torture you any longer then. I wouldn't want you to hate something I did."

She grabbed his wrist, brought it back between her thighs. "Shh."

More laughter, but he left his hand there, and by the time he turned into their driveway, the garage door opening and closing behind them, she was wet and needy and . . . she pounced on him the moment they reached the kitchen.

Fingers working his pants down.

Brit dropping to her knees.

Maybe she couldn't cook, couldn't give him a baby, couldn't make the adoption happen in the blink of an eye, but she *could* make him feel good. She could take care of his body, make him laugh, be here for him. She could love him with every part of herself, make sure he knew that.

And then they'd be okay.

And the rest of their lives would fall into place.

Six

STEFAN

"Here."

Brit plunked a present onto his lap.

It was mid-morning on Christmas Day. They'd opened everything they'd bought for each other. Or so he'd thought anyway.

But this box hadn't been under the tree.

"What is it?" he asked.

She rolled her pretty brown eyes. "If I told you, then it wouldn't be a surprise now, would it?"

He smiled at the pert tone but didn't comment, just took his time peeling up one corner of the wrapping paper printed with tiny Santa hats in a way he knew would drive her crazy. Part because they loved each other, because making each other crazy was part of that love, part because he knew that in two-point-three seconds, she would nudge the package out of his hands, plunk herself onto his lap, and start opening the present for him.

Win-win for him.

He didn't give a shit about opening presents.

He got to have his sexy wife's ass in his lap, *and* she did his dirty work for him.

"Here," she said, snagging the box and sitting down in his lap, just as he planned—muhaha—her fingers working furiously on the paper. In another two seconds, it was torn clear, the lid was open, and she slowed. "I . . ." Her chest rose and fell on a breath. She shifted off him. "Um . . . here," she murmured, handing him the box.

Heart twisting now, he took it, peered inside.

It was . . . an album.

He lifted it carefully from the box, opened the cover, and felt his heart turn over in his chest.

On the first page was the picture of them he'd printed out. Kissing and holding tight to that Christmas tree, their bodies in sync, their love written into every line of their embrace.

He ran his finger over the edge, felt the slight bump of the adhesive beneath, and then turned the page. There were pictures of them—some from the media and printed out from online like what he'd done, some actual press photos from the Gold, some selfies or posed snapshots they'd taken at different points of their relationship. They weren't arranged by date, but rather grouped together in a way that made the white spaces between them seem like part of the pattern rather than empty areas that had been neglected to be filled.

And he immediately knew what Brit had done.

Love for her was a heady thing, filling every cell to bursting, skating along his spine, so much tenderness inside him that he felt his throat grow tight.

Them.

But room to grow.

When he ran his thumb over one of those openings, struggling to control the burn in his throat, his eyes, Brit spoke. "I . . . didn't leave the space by accident. I wanted . . . well, I know it hasn't happened yet, and we both really want it to, and I just wanted you to know that when it does, there's space for us, too—"

"I know," he said, when she broke off, her throat working as he covered her hand with his. "Thank you, sweetheart."

She nodded. "I want you to know that I promise I'm going to love you better than I have. I know you've been doing a lot of the heavy lifting and that I haven't been doing enough, but I swear I'll do better—"

He placed a finger over her lips, the tenderness having faded into fury. She thought she didn't love him properly? Fucking seriously? "What the hell are you talking about?" he asked, barely restraining the urge to grab her by the shoulders and shake some sense into her. He'd ask where the hell she got that dumbass idea, except he knew the woman he loved as well as he knew the back of his hand. She had a tendency to heft too much onto her shoulders, to take the blame for every scenario on herself, whether it was because the team lost a game or . . . because she somehow thought it was her fault they didn't have a family yet.

Which . . . he realized, suddenly, was kind of what he'd been thinking.

Not that it was her fault.

But that they didn't have a family yet.

And now, seeing her there with pain in her eyes, with Brit thinking somehow she'd disappointed *him,* and he might as well have stabbed himself with his skate blade.

His wife thought she disappointed him.

Fuck.

He was an asshole.

Because they already had a family.

Because, of course, they wanted to add to it, but . . . he'd gone wrong in dwelling on what they didn't have, on the missing pieces, and he'd made his wife somehow think that she didn't love him correctly or enough or that he wasn't so fucking happy with her. His life before her had been empty.

And he'd made her think she wasn't enough.

Carefully, he set the album on the table, touched beyond words by it, but furious beyond measure with himself.

Then he took her hands in his, tugged her to her feet.

"Stef—"

He pulled her close, hearing her breath whoosh out of her. "I am so fucking sorry," he whispered, holding her as tightly as he dared.

"You don't like the album?"

His chest spasmed, and he pulled back so he could stare deeply into her eyes. "I fucking love the album."

A trickle of doubt in those chocolate depths. "I . . ."

He squeezed her hand. "Will you let me say this?"

She nodded.

"I've been focusing on everything we don't have," he said, seeing that doubt grow, coalesce, hating it with a fucking passion. "Sweetheart, I'm sorry."

Her brows drew together. "For what? I'm so busy with the team, with my sponsorships, with my training, that you do all the heavy lifting. You cook and clean. You come to every game. You fucking cue up my favorite playlist in the car. You—"

"I don't do those things because I'm making a list to compare who's doing more," he said. "I do them because I love you. That's it. It's not a tally. It's not tit for tat. I—" He cupped her cheek. "Our life isn't a scoreboard that one of us has to win, babe. It's just us and our love."

"But you do so much more than I do," she said. "You've given so much more."

Sighing, because he knew she wouldn't get it until he gave her something concrete, he sat on the couch, tugging her down beside him as he picked up the album, opening to the first page.

"Who gave me this shirt?" he asked, pointing to the picture, to the button-down she'd bought for no other reason than just because she thought he'd like it. He tapped his finger on another photo. "Who booked this concert, even though she hates live music?" Another. "Who convinced me it was a good idea to do this escape room, even though I was certain we'd totally fail and be stuck?" One more. "Who has this place decorated like Santa threw up in here?"

"You hate the decorations," she whispered.

"No," he said, stroking a finger down her cheek. "I love the way they make you smile. I love how you rearrange the ornaments on the tree a half dozen times before you're happy." She snorted, and he brought her a little closer. "For my part, maybe I don't *love* rearranging the lights, but it makes you happy—"

Brit shoved out of his arms, jumping to her feet, and his beautiful, strong wife had tears in her eyes. "Don't you see?" Her hand thumped to her chest. "Again, this has become about me. About my career. About what *I* want, what makes *me* happy."

"Baby—"

"And I'm fucking failing at being an equal partner in this!" she wailed, one tear drifting down her cheek. "You're doing everything and—" Her shoulders slumped. "And here I am, making it about me again."

He reached for her, but she dodged him, skittering back a step and knocking into the coffee table. "Sweetheart, it's—"

But then he was talking to air.

Because his wife ran out of the room.

SEVEN

BRIT

Her eyes burned, and she hated that she was upset.

More making it about herself.

"Fuck," she whispered, angrily tightening her ponytail before swiping at her eyes. "I need to stop."

"Yes."

Blinking, she turned to see Stefan stepping through the door. His face was a study of fury—sharp lines, flattened lips, a muscle twitching in his jaw. He came over to her, taking her hands in his again. "I love you," he said.

"I love you, and I'm sorry if—"

"No sorries," he interrupted. "From either of us."

She froze, lungs tight at the sharp tone.

"I can tell you that I don't give a shit about the lights, that I love looking at a hundred Christmas trees with you." His words softened. "I can tell you that when you burn dinner and get that tiny frown between your brows, my heart feels like it's grown triple in size. I don't keep an inner tally of who's loving who better, of who's doing more. You give me everything I need."

Except, she wasn't.

He sighed. "I can tell you all those things, but until you believe it in here"—he tapped her chest, just above her heart—"but no matter what I say, you're not going to listen to it."

"That's not—" She broke off, the words stumbling and tripping up in her throat, stalling as she realized that yes, he was right.

She honestly didn't feel like she was doing enough.

She honestly felt like them not having kids was all on her.

She honestly—

"Fuck," she whispered, pulling away from him, stalking across the back porch. The sky was clear and blue, the type of California Christmas she'd had years to get used to. No snow. Not even particularly chilly. In fact, the only slice of cold she had inside her was the icicle in her heart.

Because he was right.

She wouldn't believe it . . . unless *she* believed it.

Which was basically a confusing way to say that she was the type of woman that couldn't be convinced of things. She was headstrong. She liked to pave her own way—hence, the whole first woman in the NHL thing (well, technically the *second*, but she was the first to sign a contract, to play in regular-season games, to win the Cup). Anyway, the point was, many people had tried over the years to convince her that she didn't fit, that she didn't belong, that what she was doing *wasn't* enough, wouldn't *ever* be enough. And the only way she'd ever succeeded was to just put her head down and continue barreling forward.

But—she glanced up at Stefan, saw the resignation in his expression, and knew he was prepared for a fight, prepared to give her more words, more care, more . . . love.

Even though she probably wouldn't listen to any of it.

And that was a bucket of ice water pouring over her head.

Clearing her mind, knocking away the insecurity, the claws of doubt and self-loathing that had gripped her so tightly these last few weeks.

Because . . . she knew her husband.

Stefan didn't lie. Stefan didn't say things he didn't mean. Stefan had always been the most caring man she'd ever met.

So yes, it was important for her to remember that she needed to take care of him, too. But it was equally important for her to not hold tight to these doubts and insecurities. Otherwise, she was going to keep putting Stefan through the wringer.

And it wasn't his fucking job to keep reassuring her of her worth.

Sighing, she crossed to the railing, leaned back against it, her eyes drifting up, studying the barest wisps of clouds drifting across the cerulean sky.

Footsteps announced that Stefan had come over, but she would have known anyway. Because her body and soul were attuned to him, because her cells, her DNA, her very being recognized him as hers.

"Sweetheart," he murmured.

"You know," she whispered, "I once broke Blane's nose for calling me that."

"I know," he said with a laugh. "Why do you think I'm standing out of arm's reach?"

A laugh bubbled in her throat, even though it shouldn't have. She should be serious and begging for forgiveness and making all sorts of promises to not allow those doubts back in.

But . . . enough with the shoulds.

"I'm sorry," she whispered.

"I thought we said no more sorries." He slipped his arm around her waist, came close, his warm body a comfort, his scent filling her up.

"No," she told him. "*You* said that. But I didn't agree to it."

His chuckle ruffled her hair.

"Because I am sorry, I got so twisted up, and I let my insecurities take over. I'm sorry I didn't just talk about it." She spun in his arms. "And I'm sorry that you've been spinning your wheels while I've been busy with the team, and that we haven't had any calls from the adoption agency, that we haven't heard from children's services."

"But we are talking about it now, love," he murmured, smoothing her hair back. "And I know you're a perfectionist. I know you like things to work out just right"—he grinned, tugging the end of her ponytail—"because it takes a perfectionist to know a perfectionist."

She laughed. "Baby."

"Should I give you the rest of my sorries?" he asked, then didn't let her answer, just went on. "Because I'm sorry that you felt like you had to prove to me that you love me." He kissed the top of her head. "I know it. I've *known* it, and it's a gift I feel incredibly lucky to have been given. And I'm sorry, I've been playing house husband when I should have found something better to pass my time with while we wait for everything else to fall into place."

"Stefan."

He tucked her closer. "Yeah?"

"I love you."

His fingers dipped under her chin, coaxed it up. "Does this mean no more tally marks?"

How was it possible to feel this much love for another person?

"I can't make any promises," she murmured. "But I give you permission to smack me around if I start talking and thinking crazy again."

He brushed his lips across hers. "Never."

Her heart pulsed. "How about I give you permission to kiss me any time I start doubting us?"

Heat in his pale blue eyes. "*That* I could get behind."

"Stefan?"

"If it's another apology, I'm going to have to kiss you."

She wound her arms around his shoulders. "You're going to have to do that anyway." But she beat him to the punch, slanting her mouth over his, kissing him with every bit of love and affection she possessed.

Which was a whole hell of a lot.

When they broke apart, she ran her fingers through his hair.

"Was it one?" he asked.

She was still in kiss euphoria, so she asked, "Was *what* one?"

"Were you going to give me another sorry?"

No. Now she was debating dragging him upstairs and showing him all the other places she wanted him to kiss her. And considering the erection he was sporting, she didn't think it would be hard to convince him to give all those spots the attention they deserved. But before she could do that, the doorbell rang.

And she suddenly remembered what she was going to tell him.

It wasn't as fun as what she'd been fantasizing about.

But . . .

It was family.

Their family. So, it was nearly as good.

"No," she said, "I was going to remind you that your parents and our friends are going to be here any minute." It was their turn to host the gathering.

He groaned, dropped his forehead to her collarbone. "What was that about family, and why did we want one?"

She laughed, took his hand, and tugged him inside.

"Because they're fucking great, and the more, the merrier?" she said.

Stefan mock sighed. "No, definitely not that."

Another laugh, paired with so much relief that they'd talked it out, that all the sorries on both sides didn't mean their love was any less. "You're my favorite person in the whole world."

"And you, sweetheart, are mine," he murmured, cupping her cheek, his eyes warm and damp. "And it'll happen—"

"When it happens."

"And it's not—"

"My fault." She smiled and tapped her chest. "*I* know that

now. In here," she added. "It just took a while for that to sink in because I've got a thick skull."

"Thank God for that," he said, "what with all those pucks flying at you."

"I—"

The doorbell rang again.

He tapped her nose, smiled. "Later?"

She nodded. "Later." A beat. "Forever."

"Forever," he repeated.

Then they went to answer the door, and when she saw Stefan's mom and dad, Blane and Mandy, Coop and Calle, Angie and Max, and all their respective kiddos taking up space on the porch, their arms full of bottles and bags and happily wrapped presents, huge smiles on their faces, she knew, *truly* knew that they would be okay.

Because they already had their family.

And someday soon, they'd add to it.

But for now, they had enough.

Epilogue

Brit

"How about fencing?" she asked, attempting to keep a straight face.

Stefan just looked at her.

She mock sighed, tossing her pen and notebook onto the couch. "So, no knitting, no deep-sea diving, no croissant baking, no scrapbooking, no—"

He snaked an arm around her waist, yanking her up and over into his lap. His free hand slid up her side, dipping in and stopping . . . the barest inch below her aching breasts. "How about sex?" he asked, nipping at her bottom lip.

"Sex is not a hobby," she said, her hand resting on his yummy chest, her head tipping back as he dragged his mouth along her jaw, down her throat, gently grasping the sensitive spot just above her collarbone with his teeth. She shivered when his tongue darted out.

"Mmm," he said, kissing his way back up, his mouth finding hers for a brief, hot kiss. "I think I could make it one."

She thought so, too.

So long as he got his ten thousand hours of practice to become an expert with her.

And only her.

"What about painting?"

He straightened, lifting his lips from her skin, allowing her mind to clear slightly, but his expression told her that he wasn't going to pick up watercolors any time soon.

"Sara could teach you pencil drawing."

Stefan curled his lip.

She wrinkled her nose. "You're difficult." He kept his arm around her while he pulled out his phone. "What are you doing?"

"I'm researching."

Her brow creased. "Researching what?"

"Sex."

"Um, what?"

"If my hobby is going to be sex," he said, scrolling through the online retailer on his cell, "I need to be an expert."

"With me?"

His blue eyes flashed to hers, one corner of his mouth tipping up. He tapped her on the nose. "And only you."

This she was fine with. Snuggling up next to him, she turned her eyes toward the TV, toward the documentary on glass blowing that she'd put on before they'd begun their discussion— and continued her obsession—to find Stefan a hobby.

She'd thrown pretty much any activity she could think of at him. Hell, some of those endeavors she'd bandied his way more than once.

Crafting was out. Cooking and baking, too. He hated golf and wasn't interested in picking up another sport. God knew, he'd spent enough time playing hockey.

Hockey.

Hockey.

"What about coaching?" she asked, straightening and spinning to face him.

He was already shaking his head. "The Gold's staff is great already—"

"No." She clambered onto his lap. "Fanny was just telling me today that one of the Junior Gold teams' coaches had to move, and they didn't have anyone to fill in."

"But I've never coached," he said.

"But," she countered, "you spent many years *being* coached. You know what makes a good one and what makes a bad one. You know what it is to be a player. And," she said, smoothing a hand down his chest, "you have the skills. All you'd have to do is share them."

"Hmm."

This time it wasn't a delaying sound.

"How old are they?"

She smiled, feeling victory on the horizon. "8Us."

His eyes were unfocused, his mind far away as he considered. "I'm not sure I'd be any good at it."

Her heart pulsed. God, she loved this man. "You will be," she said. "And even if you were shit in the beginning, you'd learn."

His lips parted.

"The kids need you," she whispered.

He nodded.

And she knew they'd found it.

The missing piece he'd been looking for.

He'd be an amazing coach.

Which was why she pulled out *her* cell, texted Fanny, and volunteered Stefan for the job. Then she snagged *his* phone, filled his cart with all the supplies he'd need to be the best 8U coach in the history of all 8U coaches.

But—just for the record—when she hit the purchase button, the books he'd picked out were still in the cart.

There wasn't any reason Stefan couldn't have *two* hobbies.

Epilogue

Brit was snoring softly next to him, her naked, lithe body scantily covered by a sheet, proof of how good he'd gotten at a certain hobby.

His other had gone well, too.

His 8Us had won the State Championships before getting knocked out in Regionals.

Still, not bad for his first foray in coaching.

The girls had run him ragged, twisted him around their tiny, little fingers so effectively that he'd taken them all for end-of-season pedicures—and then go-carting because they were girls and they could do anything they wanted, whether it was picking out Stefan's pink nail polish or blowing by him on the course.

Brit had been right. Coaching was freaking awesome, and he'd loved every minute of practice, off-ice, and game play. Though his heart had broken right along with theirs when they'd lost that final game at Regionals.

He'd been equally as devastated at that loss as when the Gold had lost the Cup.

Still, the girls were receptive, smart, energetic, and getting so damned skilled that he knew they'd become formidable players as they continued honing their abilities.

And he looked forward to continuing to hone his coaching skills on them.

Poor babies.

He was already planning drills for next year—and some of those included help from the skating guru herself, Fanny.

Grinning, he shifted, resting his head back on the pillow and closing his eyes.

It had just ticked past midnight and the stars were out, the night filled with the promise of something intangible, even though the other bedrooms in their house were still empty.

They hadn't been empty the entire seven months.

They'd been lucky enough to be home to a brother and sister, ages four and eight, for two months while their mom had needed a chance to get back up on her feet. It was one of the most rewarding experiences of his life, being able to help someone.

But . . .

It had torn his heart out when they'd left.

And Brit hadn't been in any better shape.

They'd both cried like babies, even though Kyle and Lee and their mom, Cherice, were now part of their extended family. She'd become a friend and sent them regular pictures from their new place in San Diego with her mom. So, it wasn't like it was across the world, just a few hundred miles.

But the experience had been enough for them to know that they couldn't do it.

They didn't have the strength to allow kids into their lives and to let them go, over and over again. They were still on the registry, their license had been approved, and their home would always be available for emergencies, but they couldn't do it day-by-day and maintain their sanity.

It was just too hard.

So, in many ways, they were back to waiting for the adoption agency to make a match.

And two months had turned into nine, to almost ten.

Still not an eternity, but it certainly felt like one.

Sighing, he settled deeper into the pillows, having found the patience to let life unfold as an early Christmas present, and when that patience waned, finding it bolstered by Brit.

The sorries were gone.

The season was over.

Hobbies had been found.

They were leaving in a few days for two weeks of vacation on the beach.

Life was perfect.

He smiled, tugged the covers up, let sleep come . . .

Until his phone buzzed with a text.

Blearily, he picked it up off the nightstand. Only one number wasn't on Do Not Disturb—their contact at the adoption agency.

He swiped at the screen, opened the message.

Then dropped the phone, spending several moments scrambling to grab it off the floor, his hands shaking, the words seemingly unbelievable. He read it several more times, just to be sure before he woke his slumbering wife.

Because, holy shit, he and Brit . . .

They'd just gotten the best present of their lives.

Christmas in July.

Guess they weren't taking that beach vacation after all.

———

CHARLIE

He wove his way through the bowels of the arena, waiting for Fanny or Scar or Kaydon or Mandy.

Or any of the people he wanted to see.

As opposed to the one person he was trying to *avoid* seeing.

Ji-Ho.

His ex had taken a transfer and was now working in the San Francisco office, and...he was at the Gold game that evening.

In the company box.

Charlie hadn't been there, thankfully, even though he worked for the same company, the same branch. Even though he'd worked with Ji-Ho in Korea—

Love. A broken heart. Despair. Now...alone. So *fucking* alone.

Needless to say, he'd been avoiding Ji-Ho since he'd heard of his ex's transfer.

But that wasn't why he hadn't been in the Steele Technologies box. His sister worked for the Gold, so he usually sat in the team box when he came to catch a game, watching her do her publicist thing, smiling as she mooned over her gorgeous hockey player man...*fiancé?*

He wasn't quite sure where they stood. Kaydon never took off a plastic Hello Kitty ring his sister had proposed with, but Scar wasn't sporting a diamond, and though they'd moved in together, neither of them appeared to be moving toward setting any wedding dates.

It was just...a love fest.

All the time.

His friend—and former date (*one* date, but still)—Fanny, and her husband Brandon. Scar and Kaydon. Mandy and Blane. Brit and Stefan. Coop and Calle. Char and Logan. Dani and Ethan. Mia and—

Well, the point was that there weren't a lot of prospects for a single man on this team.

Even less so when he considered that none of the single men were bi or gay or interested in a semi-scrawny (at least compared to them) redhead bisexual man who'd had his heart broken and had run away like a baby because of it. *And* all the women he knew were paired up.

Because if they were single and interested, he would be *such* a catch, right?

Right.

And yes, that was sarcasm.

So anyway, he'd been sitting on the chair next to Scar, amazed at all the things she did at once and handled with aplomb, and he'd turned, and...

Ji-Ho.

In the next box over.

Charlie had wanted to run, to hide, to pretend he hadn't seen his ex.

But...pride.

So, he had lifted his chin, held his stare steady when their eyes had locked, and...he'd pretended that his heart wasn't still cracked.

Still shattered.

It wouldn't have worked out. He knew that now. But, fuck, he'd moved halfway around the world to be closer to the man he'd met at a conference, a man he'd thought might be something permanent, and they'd ended up...

As a disaster.

He'd moved home.

Now Ji-Ho was here. *Why* was he here?

Charlie wasn't about to find out. Not when the man had cheated on him. Not when he'd sabotaged Charlie's work. Not when...he hadn't treated Charlie's heart with the same care every couple in this strange cornucopia of happy endings treated their partners' hearts.

He wanted *that.*

Care.

To receive. To give.

And he deserved it.

"*I* deserve it," he whispered, pushing through the door to a room that was usually empty, intending to take a moment to get that sentiment through his thick, still-sort-of-pining-for-Ji-Ho-even-though-that-was-fucking-stupid-because-Ji-Ho-was-a-creep skull.

However, instead of making his way through the door, he collided with something firm and huge...

And gold.

No *Gold*. As in, Goldie.

The #GlitteryGoldieGuano.

The giant poop-shaped mascot that had somehow become—much to Scar's chagrin—a fan-favorite. With their collision, the poop—well, the costume performer—tipped over backward, landing with an *oof* that made Charlie cringe and rush forward, kneeling at the glittering dump's side.

The triangular piece at the top had popped off, rolled across the room.

"Are you oka—"

His words froze in his throat. His heart seized.

Because the top of that giant golden poop had fallen off and revealed...

The most beautiful woman he'd ever seen.

———

Thank you for reading! I hope you loved revisiting Stefan and Brit as much as I did! The next book in the Gold Hockey series is CAUGHT.

She'd thought he was going to ask her to fix his computer. Instead, he'd asked her *out*.

CLICK HERE TO READ CAUGHT NOW>

And if you enjoyed A Gold Christmas, you'll love the sexy, sweet, and close-knit Breakers Hockey crew. The first book in the series, BROKEN, is now live!

Her life was a disaster...Don't miss the hilarious Life Sucks series, starting with TRAIN WRECK. Derek Cashette was determined to salvage the train wreck of her life...and she was just as determined *not* to let him be the hero.

DOWNLOAD TRAIN WRECK FOR FREE at
www.elisefaber.com/train-wreck

I so appreciate your help in spreading the word about my books,
including sharing with friends! Please leave a review on your
favorite book site!
You can also join my Facebook group, the Fabinators, for exclusive
giveaways and sneak peeks of future books.

SIGN UP FOR ELISE FABER'S NEWSLETTER HERE:
https://www.elisefaber.com/newsletter

———

Want a free bonus story? Hate missing Elise's new releases? Love contests, exclusive excerpts and giveaways?
Then signup for Elise's newsletter here!
https://www.elisefaber.com/newsletter

———

And join Elise's fan group, the Fabinators https://www.facebook.com/groups/fabinators for insider information, sneak peaks at new releases, and fun freebies! Hope to see you there!

Gold Hockey Series

GOLD HOCKEY

Did you miss any of the Gold Hockey books?
Find information about the full series here.
Or keep reading for a sneak peek into each of the books below!

Blocked
Gold Hockey Book #1
Get your copy at https://www.elisefaber.com/blocked

BRIT

The first question Brit always got when people found out she played ice hockey was *"Do you have all of your teeth?"* The second was *"Do you, you know, look at the guys in the locker room?"*

The first she could deal with easily—flash a smile of her full set of chompers, no gaps in sight. The second was more problematic. Especially since it was typically accompanied by a smug smile or a coy wink.

Of course she looked. *Everybody* looked once. Everyone snuck a glance, made a judgment that was quickly filed away and shoved deep down into the recesses of their mind.

And she meant *way* down.

Because, dammit, she was there to play hockey, not assess her teammates' six packs. If she wanted to get her man candy fix, she could just go on social media. There were shirtless guys for days filling her feed.

But that wasn't the answer the media wanted.

Who cared about locker room dynamics? Who gave a damn whether or not she, as a typical heterosexual woman, found her fellow players attractive?

Yet for some inane reason, it *did* matter to people.

Brit wasn't stupid. The press wanted a story. A scandal. They were desperate for her to fall for one of her teammates—or better yet the captain from their rival team—and have an affair that was worthy of a romantic comedy.

She'd just gotten very good at keeping her love life—as nonexistent as it was—to herself, gotten very good at not reacting in any perceptible way to the insinuations.

So when the reporter asked her the same set of questions for the thousandth time in her twenty-six years, she grinned—showing off those teeth—and commented with a sweetly innocent "Could've sworn you were going to ask me about the coed showers." She waited for the room-at-large to laugh then said, "Next question, please."

–Get your copy at https://www.elisefaber.com/blocked

Backhand
Gold Hockey Book #2
Get your copy at https://www.elisefaber.com/backhand

Sara

"Sorry I messed up your sketch," he rumbled.

She nibbled on the side of her mouth, biting back a smile. "Sorry I stole your hand for so long."

He shrugged. "My mom's an artist. I get it."

Well, there went her battle with the smile. Her lips twitched and her teeth came out of hiding. If there was one thing that Sara had, it was her smile. It had been her trademark in her competition days.

Which were long over.

Her mouth flattened out, the grin slipping away. Time to go, time to forget, to move on, to rebuild. "Thanks," she said and extended a hand.

Then winced and dropped it when her ribs cried out in protest.

"You okay?" he asked, head tilting, eyes studying her.

"Fine." And out popped her new smile. The fake one. Careful of her aching side, she shrugged into her backpack. "I've got to go." She turned, ponytail flapping through the hair to land on her opposite shoulder.

"That—" He touched her arm. "Wait. I *know* I know you."

She froze. That was the second time he'd said that, and now they were getting into dangerous territory. Recognition meant . . . no. She couldn't.

There had been a time when *everyone* had known her. Her face on Wheaties boxes, her smile promoting toothpaste and credit cards alike.

That wasn't her life any longer.

"Thanks again. Bye." She started to hurry away.

"Wait." A hand dropped on to her shoulder, thwarting her escape, and she hissed in pain.

"Sorry," he said, but he didn't release her. Instead, he shifted his grip from her aching shoulder down to her elbow and when she didn't protest, he exerted gentle pressure until Sara was facing him again. "It's just that know I *know* you."

No. This wasn't happening.

"You're Sara Jetty."

Her body went tense.

Oh God. This was *so* happening.

"It's me." He touched his chest like she didn't know he was talking about himself, and even as she was finally recognizing the color of his eyes, the familiar curve of his lips and line of his jaw, he said the worst thing ever, "Mike Stewart."

Oh *shit*.

—Get your copy at https://www.elisefaber.com/backhand

Boarding

Gold Hockey Book #3

Get your copy at https://www.elisefaber.com/boarding

MANDY

Hockey players had the *best* asses.

No pancake bottoms, these men—and *women*—could fill out a pair of jeans. She wanted to squeeze it, to nibble it, bounce a dime—

Mandy dropped her chin to her chest, losing sight of the Sorting Hat cupcakes she'd been pondering.

Blane with his yummy ass had a unique way of distracting her.

No, it wasn't even distraction, per se. He had *always* been able to get under her skin.

And that was very, very bad for her.

"Ugh," she said, tossing her phone onto her desk and standing, knowing that she wouldn't be able to sit still now.

Nope, she needed about forty laps in the pool and a good hard fu—

Run, her mind blurted, almost yelling at the mental voice of her inner devil. *A good hard run.*

Unfortunately, the cajoling tone wasn't completely drowned out. *Some sexy horizontal time with Blane would be more fun—*

But the rest of the enticing words were lost as the roar of the crowd suddenly penetrated through the layers of concrete. Her stomach twisted. Mandy could tell, even before her eyes made it to the television, that it wasn't in celebration of a goal or a good hit either.

This was fury, a collective of outrage.

She was on her feet the moment she saw the prone form lying so still face down on the ice.

Her gut twisted when she spotted the curving line of a numeral two on the back of the player's jersey.

"Not him," she said and the words were familiar, a sentiment she had whispered, had *prayed* a thousand times before. She needed the camera angle to shift, for her to be able to see more clearly *who* was hurt. "Not him."

Then Dr. Carter was on the ice and the player moved slightly, rolling away from the camera, giving a full shot of his back and the matching twos adorning his jersey.

Fuck. Not him. Not Blane.

And that was when she saw the pool of blood.

—Get your copy at https://www.elisefaber.com/boarding

Benched
Gold Hockey Book #4
Get your copy at https://www.elisefaber.com/benched

MAX

He started up the car, listening and chiming in at the right places as Brayden talked all things video game.

But his mind was unfortunately stuck on the fact that women were not to be trusted.

He snorted. Brit—the Gold's goalie and the first female in the NHL—and Mandy—the team's head trainer—would smack him around for that sentiment, so he silently amended it to: *most* women were not to be trusted.

There. Better, see?

Somehow, he didn't think they'd see.

He parked in the school's lot, walked Brayden in, and received the appropriate amount of scorn from the secretary for being thirty minutes late to school, then bent to hug Brayden.

"I'll pick you up today," he said.

Brayden smiled and hugged him tightly. Then he whispered something in his ear that hit Max harder than a two-by-four to the temple.

"If you got me a new mom, we wouldn't be late for school."

"Wh-what?" Max stammered.

"Please, Dad? Can you?"

And with that mind fuck of an ask, Brayden gave him one more squeeze and pushed through the door to the playground, calling, "Love you!" over his shoulder.

Then he was gone, and Max was standing in the office of his son's school struggling to comprehend if he had actually just heard what he'd heard.

A new mom?

Fuck his life.

—Get your copy at https://www.elisefaber.com/benched

Breakaway
Gold Hockey Book #5
Get your copy at https://www.elisefaber.com/breakaway

BLUE

"Thanks for the ride."

"Try not to go out and get a fresh bimbo to ride tonight. I hear STIs on are the rise in the city."

Blue sighed, turned back to face her. "Really?"

She shrugged, smirk teasing the edges of her mouth, drawing his focus to the lushness of her lips. "Just watching out for Max's teammate."

He rolled his eyes. "Not hardly."

"Okay, how about I'm trying to prevent you from spreading STIs to the female populace."

"I'm clean, and I'm smart," he told her. "Condoms all the way."

"Ew."

Except there was something about the way she said it that made Blue stiffen and take notice. Because . . . he stared into her eyes, watched as the pale blue darkened to royal, saw her lips part, and her suck in a breath.

Holy shit.

"You're attracted to me."

Her jaw dropped. "No fucking way," she said, too quickly, pink dancing on the edges of her cheekbones. "You're delusional."

Blue got close.

Real close.

Anna licked her lips.

And fuck it all, he kissed that luscious mouth.

—Breakaway, https://www.elisefaber.com/breakaway

Breakout
Gold Hockey Book #6
Get your copy at https://www.elisefaber.com/breakout

PR-REBECCA

A fucking perfect hockey fairy tale.

Shaking her head, because she knew firsthand that fairy tales didn't exist outside of rom-coms and occasionally between alpha sports heroes and their chosen mates, Rebecca slipped through the corridor and stepped onto the Gold's bench.

Lots of dudes in suits—of both the boardroom *and* the hockey variety—were hugging.

On the ice. Near the goals. On the bench.

It was a proverbial hug-fest.

And she was the cynical bitch who couldn't enjoy the fact

that the team she was with had just won the biggest hockey prize of them all.

"I knew you'd be like this."

Rebecca turned her focus from Brit, who was skating with the huge silver cup, to the man—no, to the *boy* because no matter how pretty and yummy he was, Kevin was still a decade younger than her—leaning oh so casually against the boards.

"Nice goal," she told him.

A shrug. "Blue made a nice pass."

And dammit, the fact that he wasn't an arrogant son of a bitch made her like him more.

She nodded at the cup. "You should go have your turn."

"I'll get mine," he said with another shrug.

She frowned, honestly confused. "You don't want—"

Suddenly he was in front of her on the bench, towering over her even though she was wearing her four-inch power heels. "You know what I want?"

Rebecca couldn't speak. Her breath had whooshed out of her in the presence of all that sweaty, hockey god-ness. Fuck he was pretty and gorgeous and . . . so fucking masculine that her thighs actually clenched together.

She wanted to climb him like a stripper pole.

"Do you?" he asked again when her words wouldn't come. "Want to know what I want?"

She nodded.

He bent, lips to her ear. "You, babe," he whispered. "I. Want. You."

Then he straightened and jumped back onto the ice, leaving her gaping after him like she had less than two brain cells in her skull.

The worst part?

She wanted him, too.

Had wanted him since the moment she'd laid eyes on the sexy as sin hockey god.

"Trouble," she murmured. "I'm in *so* much fucking trouble."

—Breakout, https://www.elisefaber.com/breakout

Checked

Gold Hockey Book #7

Get your copy at https://www.elisefaber.com/checked

"Rebecca."

She kept walking.

She might work with Gabe, but she sure as heck wasn't on speaking terms with him. He'd dismissed her work, ignored her contribution to the team. He'd made her feel small and unimportant and—

She kept walking.

"*Rebecca.*"

Not happening. Her car was in sight, thank fuck. She beeped the locks, reached for the handle.

He caught her arm.

"Baby—"

"I am *not* your baby, and you don't get to touch me." She ripped herself free, started muttering as she reached for the handle of her car again. "You don't even like me."

He stepped close, real close. Not touching her, not pushing the boundary she'd set, and yet he still got really freaking close. Her breath caught, her chin lifted, her pulse picked up. "That. Is. Where. You're. Wrong."

She froze.

"What?"

His mouth dropped to her ear, still not touching, but near enough that she could feel his hot breath.

"I like you, Rebecca. Too fucking much."

Then he turned and strode away.

—Checked, https://www.elisefaber.com/checked

Coasting
Gold Hockey Book #8
Get your copy at https://www.elisefaber.com/coasting

Coop

Without thinking, he caught her arm.

"You're not okay."

She shuddered to a stop when he touched her, not fighting the grip, chin dropping to her chest. "No," she said, "you're right. I'm not okay."

"Who was on the phone?" he asked gently.

Her jaw went tight. "My ex."

Fury blazed through him. "Did he hurt you?" he growled.

A shake of her head. "Not like you're thinking." She sucked in a breath. "He broke my heart."

Coop's own heart gave a twinge. "I'm sorry, Calle. That's—"

"Fucking stupid." Another tear joined the first, dripping down the pale skin of her cheek.

"It's not stupid to have loved someone," he said gently.

Her eyes went fierce. "It's incredibly stupid when the person who supposedly loves you right back doesn't give a damn that you're pregnant."

His jaw fell open. He knew it did.

But Calle? Even, gentle *Calle* had gotten knocked up and—

"Yup," she said, brushing by him. "See? Really *fucking* stupid."

And without another word, she disappeared into the rink.

—Coasting, https://www.elisefaber.com/coasting

Centered
Gold Hockey Book #9
Get your copy at https://www.elisefaber.com/centered

"Watch out!"

The warning came a second too late.

He'd already stepped off the curb, already put himself in range of the car that was blowing through the red light, tearing through the intersection, not giving a shit that there were pedestrians walking—

Well, of all the ways to go, at least this would be quick.

But just as the car came within an inch of him, Liam found himself jerked back onto the curb, his one-hundred-and-eighty-pound frame becoming unwieldy and clumsy.

Kind of like on the ice over the last few years.

That was his last thought before he found himself sprawled, ass first, on the San Franciscan sidewalk.

Gross.

"What. The. *Fuck?*" a female voice snapped.

The same female voice that had warned him.

"Do you have a fucking death wish?" she yelled, causing his eyes to snap open, making him look up at an angel . . . a foot tapping, arms crossed, seriously pissed, and seemingly way too small to have been able to haul his ass back onto the curb female.

Liam thought he just might have that death wish.

Especially if it meant he got to be rescued by a woman who looked like an angel. He opened his mouth to reply.

But apparently didn't work fast enough.

Because the woman, the beautiful, curvy female, made a disgusted noise and strode away from him.

He watched her go, watched that gorgeous ass stride down the sidewalk, and stop outside a storefront.

And suddenly, he thought that, hockey or not, he might just want to stay in San Francisco after all.

—Centered, https://www.elisefaber.com/centered

Charging
Gold Hockey Book #10

Get your copy at https://www.elisefaber.com/charging

"Your feet hurt."

Her brows drew together. "What?"

Logan nodded at her feet, clad in a lovely pair of heels that, while beautiful, were also the equivalent of bear traps—and if that wasn't the perfect metaphor for the man in front of her, she didn't know what was.

"Those heels hurt you." His head tilted to the side. "Why do you wear them?"

She scoffed. "None of your fucking business, Walker."

A smile—slow and hot and sliding like silk over her breasts, her stomach, between her legs. "I knew you'd say that."

"I—"

He held up a box she hadn't noticed, pushed it into her hands when she stepped back. "Open it," he said, voice dropping and joining that silk of his smile to dip between her legs. "If you think you can handle it."

And then he was gone, the door closing behind him, leaving her with a heavy ass bag packed with who knew what, aching feet, and a box in her hands.

A box given on a challenge.

A box he knew she'd open.

Because Charlotte Harris didn't give in or back down. She liked that even less than she liked losing.

So, she opened the lid.

And instantly knew she was in trouble.

—Charging, https://www.elisefaber.com/charging

Caged
Gold Hockey Book #11
Get your copy at https://www.elisefaber.com/caged

"Are you seeing anyone?"

Slowly, she spun back, eyes wide.

"That was my question," he said, when she stared at him in shock. "Dani?" he asked, when she just continued staring at him mutely. "Did I break you?"

A slow shake of her head.

He stepped a little closer, just near enough that she could feel the heat from his body. "No to the breaking you part, or no to the seeing anyone piece?" he murmured.

"The seeing anyone thing," she somehow managed to whisper, despite the fact that the question from a man like him to a woman like her was absolutely one hundred percent unfathomable.

Circling back to sad and single and—

He smiled.

And she actually felt her brain cells collide and fizzle into smoke. That smile was dangerous, could without a doubt, turn her stupid. *Really* stupid.

"Good," he murmured.

Swallowing hard, she nodded, cheeks on fire, and turned away again. "Right, I'll just—"

"Will you go out with me?"

Her fingers went limp. The tablets hit the ground.

This time, the *crunch* sounded much more ominous.

Or maybe that was just her heart.

—Caged, https://www.elisefaber.com/caged

Also by Elise Faber

Billionaire's Club (all stand alone)

Bad Night Stand

Bad Breakup

Bad Husband

Bad Hookup

Bad Divorce

Bad Fiancé

Bad Boyfriend

Bad Blind Date

Bad Wedding

Bad Engagement

Bad Bridesmaid

Bad Swipe

Bad Girlfriend

Bad Best Friend

Bad Billionaire's Quickies

Gold Hockey (all stand alone)

Blocked

Backhand

Boarding

Benched

Breakaway

Breakout

Checked

Coasting

Centered

Charging

Caged

Crashed

A Gold Christmas

Cycled

Caught

Cap

Breakers Hockey (all stand alone)

Broken

Boldly

Breathless

Ballsy

Bewitched

Love, Action, Camera (all stand alone)

Dotted Line

Action Shot

Close-Up

End Scene

Meet Cute

Love After Midnight (all stand alone)

Rum And Notes

Virgin Daiquiri

On The Rocks

Sex On The Seats

Life Sucks Series (all stand alone)

Train Wreck

Hot Mess

Dumpster Fire

Clusterf*@k

FUBAR (March 29,2022)

Roosevelt Ranch Series (all stand alone, series complete)

Disaster at Roosevelt Ranch

Heartbreak at Roosevelt Ranch

Collision at Roosevelt Ranch

Regret at Roosevelt Ranch

Desire at Roosevelt Ranch

Phoenix Series (read in order)

Phoenix Rising

Dark Phoenix

Phoenix Freed

Phoenix: LexTal Chronicles (rereleasing soon, stand alone, Phoenix world)

From Ashes

In Flames

To Smoke

KTS Series

Riding The Edge

Crossing The Line

Leveling The Field

Scorching The Earth

Cocky Heroes World

Tattooed Troublemaker

About the Author

USA Today bestselling author, Elise Faber, loves chocolate, Star Wars, Harry Potter, and hockey (the order depending on the day and how well her team -- the Sharks! -- are playing). She and her husband also play as much hockey as they can squeeze into their schedules, so much so that their typical date night is spent on the ice. Elise changes her hair color more often than some people change their socks, loves sparkly things, and is the mom to two exuberant boys. She lives in Northern California. Connect with her in her Facebook group, the Fabinators or find more information about her books at www.elisefaber.com.

facebook.com/elisefaberauthor

amazon.com/author/elisefaber

bookbub.com/profile/elise-faber

instagram.com/elisefaber

goodreads.com/elisefaber

pinterest.com/elisefaberwrite

www.ingramcontent.com/pod-product-compliance
Lightning Source LLC
Chambersburg PA
CBHW071135100726
47908CB00008B/2604